Michael Crowley is a  written for the stage, teaches creative writi University and was w HM YOI Lancaster Farms between 2007 and 2013. He has previously worked in youth justice as a restorative justice coordinator. He is the author of *Behind the Lines: Creative writing with offenders and people at risk* (Waterside Press, 2012) and in 2013 he was shortlisted for a Butler Trust Award for services to criminal justice in regard to his writing work with prisoners.

About Diffusion books

Diffusion publishes books for adults who are emerging readers. There are two series:

 Books in the Diamond series are ideally suited to those who are relatively new to reading or who have not practised their reading skills for some time (approximately Entry Level 2 to 3 in adult literacy levels).

 Books in the Star series are for those who are ready for the next step. These books will help to build confidence and inspire readers to tackle longer books (approximately Entry Level 3 to Level 1 in adult literacy levels).

Other books available in the Star series are:

Not Such a Bargain by Toby Forward

Barcelona Away by Tom Palmer

Forty-six Quid and a Bag of Dirty Washing by Andy Croft

Bare Freedom by Andy Croft

One Shot by Lena Semaan

NOWHERE TO RUN

MICHAEL CROWLEY

diffusion

First published in Great Britain in 2016

Diffusion
an imprint of
SPCK
36 Causton Street
London
SW1P 4ST
www.spck.org.uk

ISBN 978–1–908713–05–6
e-Book ISBN 978–1–908713–19–3

Typeset by Graphicraft Limited, Hong Kong
First printed in Great Britain by Ashford Colour Press
Subsequently digitally reprinted in Great Britain

Produced on paper from sustainable forests

*Dedicated to the memory of
James Ruse (1759–1837),
Australia's pioneer farmer*

For Ben

Contents

1

Nowhere to run

Jacob Jones stood perfectly still. He watched the brown snake move forward across the red earth. As it got close to Jacob, it stopped. Perhaps it could tell something was not right. In that split second Jacob brought his hatchet down with full force and cut the snake's head off. He held the snake up by the tail and the men around him gave a cheer. Private Duggan walked over to Jacob, carrying his musket with him.

'Give it to me,' said Duggan.

'I killed it, boss. I should have it,' complained Jacob.

'You know the Governor's orders. Any animals killed have to be shared,' said Duggan.

Private Duggan snatched the snake off Jacob. He took it over to the shade of a gum tree and placed it in his canvas backpack. Jacob and the half-dozen other convicts standing in the blazing sun watched him. Snake meat was a good meal. It tasted like chicken.

It was a lot better than the usual food the convicts were given.

'Back to work!' shouted Duggan.

Jacob and the other convicts picked up their spades and went back to breaking the hard, dry ground. Duggan watched them as he lit his pipe. He had been a marine for twenty years and been halfway round the world to fight wars for Britain. But he thought Australia was the strangest place he had ever set foot in. Still, it was an easy job. There was no army to fight, just a few natives to scare now and again. It was just what he wanted at his time of life.

Jacob wondered why Duggan bothered guarding the convicts. None of them would try to run away because there was nowhere to run to. Beyond the settlement, there was just the wilderness and the natives. For this was New South Wales, Australia, in the year 1788. The men and women here were either prisoners or guards.

In the 1780s, England only had a few jails and they were full to bursting. People were hanged, even for crimes like stealing a loaf of bread. But the fear of execution did not stop people from breaking the law. They were desperate, poor and hungry, and sometimes crime seemed the only answer. So the government came up with a plan to sort out the problem of overcrowded jails. They decided to send the criminals to the other end of the world. Jacob and eight hundred other prisoners had been transported to Australia to serve their time. And serving your time meant building a settlement and being guarded by marines. It was hard labour in hot weather.

Jacob and a few other convicts were clearing ground for a farm, a mile from the camp. The area was chosen because of a stream. Jacob was chosen because he had been a farmer. He had begun working on farms as a child when he would scare crows from crops for a few pennies. He was now twenty-five and knew a thing or two about farming

He knew that the soil they were working, in New South Wales, was useless. He bent down and smelt the earth. He felt it between his fingers. It was nothing like the rich soil back home. If there was to be any chance of a crop growing it would need a lot of graft. But the other men he was working with knew nothing about farming. They were the dregs of London mostly. Cut-throats, pickpockets, or just plain poor and hungry.

Jacob watched a scrawny boy tickle the ground with a hoe. His name was Barrett.

He was only about seventeen years old. Jacob had heard he was a forger and a lock picker. He was also a coiner. He had been transported for making fake coins. It was said that on the boat from England Barrett had turned brass buttons and belt buckles into coins and then passed them off to marines for extra rations.

'Barrett, you think you're going to feed yourself working like that?' asked Jacob.

Barrett stood straight. His eyes were fearless. He was skinny but he was already as tall as Jacob. He looked over at Duggan who was watching the trees for a bird to shoot and walked over to Jacob.

'I'll feed myself, don't you worry,' said Barrett, pressing his sharp nose against Jacob's face. 'And you're not the gaffer. So forget about giving me orders.'

Barrett spat on the ground and turned away. He may have been skinny but he was not to be crossed. He was as crafty as a fox.

Jacob did not trust coiners. It was a coiner who had got him arrested. Near where Jacob lived in England was a man who was forging coins. Jacob had been desperate for money. He had rent to pay and his wife was expecting their first baby. So he went to the coiner's house to look for his hoard of coins. He did not find the coins but on the kitchen table he saw a silver watch. He picked it up and smiled to himself. Then he felt the coiner's pistol on the back of his head and heard the click of the hammer.

At Jacob's trial the coiner had come across as an honest man of business. There was no mention of the fake coins he had made. Jacob could have been sentenced to death – people were hanged for less serious crimes than his – but instead he was sentenced to transportation for seven years.

After two weeks working in the burning heat of a New South Wales summer, Jacob's blond hair had bleached almost to white and his skin had turned red. He hacked away at a vine that covered the ground. There were gum trees standing every ten yards or so, like grey pillars. A beetle crawled out from under a leaf. It had white spots on its back and was like a walking dice. Jacob thought about picking it up but both convicts and marines had been bitten by insects and taken sick.

Then one of the strange creatures some of the other men had talked about appeared on the edge of the woods. It stood upright on its hind legs and had a sheep's face.

It had ears like a donkey. Some of the men called these animals 'kangaroos'. The kangaroo watched the men and sniffed the air. Duggan picked up his musket but before he could take aim the animal jumped back into the woods.

Barrett walked over to Duggan and asked for a drink from the water barrel. There were set water breaks but Barrett always wanted more than his share. Duggan was waving him away when a spear flew past Barrett and went straight through Duggan's leg, pinning him to the tree.

'Natives!' someone shouted.

Two convicts dropped their tools and began running back to the camp. Out of the woods appeared three tall native men. They were armed with clubs and spears. One of them jumped forward onto one foot and launched his spear into the back of a fleeing convict. The convict fell to the ground without a sound.

Duggan pulled at the spear in his leg, screaming, 'Get it out, get it out!'

Barrett had run to the centre of the cleared ground. Perhaps he thought they were surrounded. Jacob and another man, William Davies, joined Barrett. They stood back to back in a defensive triangle. Two of the native men, armed with clubs, stood tall and fearless staring at the three convicts.

'Jacob, give me your hatchet,' Davies said, holding out his hand.

Jacob didn't argue. Davies was a hot-tempered man from Cornwall. He had flaming red hair and was as broad as a barrel. He stepped forward swinging the hatchet.

'Come on, then,' Davies said with a snarl. 'Which one of you wants to dance?'

He tossed the hatchet from one hand to the other. His blood was up. He was about to make his move when a native woman appeared. She stood between Davies and the men with clubs.

'Waroo, waroo,' she cried, waving a stick in Davies's face.

Jacob had no idea what the word meant but the natives retreated back into the woods. Davies turned and laughed. Jacob ran over to Duggan and eased the point of the spear out of the tree. He then broke its shaft. Duggan cried out in agony, clutching at what remained of the spear in his leg.

Meanwhile Davies had taken the bayonet off Duggan's musket.

'We can bury the bayonet and the hatchet here,' he whispered to Barrett. 'Tell the Governor that the natives stole them.'

Davies and Barrett ran to a corner of the cleared ground and buried the hatchet and the bayonet by the trunk of a gum tree.

Jacob was half-carrying Duggan in the direction of the camp.

'One of you, help me,' he called out. 'We need to get him to the surgeon.'

An hour later the four of them staggered into the main camp of the settlement called Sydney.

What do you think?

Why do you think Davies has hidden the hatchet and bayonet?

How do you think Jacob and the other convicts felt about being transported to Australia? Was it better or worse than being sent to jail or even hanged in England?

What do you think about the idea that prisoners today could be made to work as part of their sentence?

2

The price of promotion

Early the following morning the Governor
called everyone together. Marines and convicts
stood on the beach in ranks under the burning
February sun. The Union Jack fluttered in the
breeze. The Governor was dressed in his royal
blue coat and was standing on a box. He was
tall and thin, an old man who rarely smiled.
It had taken many months at sea to get to
Australia and the journey had aged him.

'I wanted to talk to you all this morning,' he
said. 'Many of you will be wondering about food.
I can tell you that we have brought enough
supplies to last to the end of the year. After that
we must grow our own food. If we don't, we
shall starve. We must all work together. So I have
decided that we will all have the same rations.
From now on, convicts, marines and officers
will all be given the same amount of food.'

There were some complaints from the marines.

'Quiet in the ranks,' the Governor snapped.
'We cannot go on if there is further stealing.

From now on, anyone stealing food will be hanged. There is no other way that this settlement will survive.'

The convicts divided up into their work parties. There was a saw pit and a new clay pit where they were making bricks. Women convicts were collecting oyster shells to burn for the lime. Jacob stood with Barrett and Davies.

'Suppose we had better get off to our so-called farm,' said Jacob.

'Not me,' said Davies, smiling. 'I've got myself on the fishing crew now.'

Barrett laughed. 'You can bring us back a fish,' he said.

Davies moved in closer to the other two.

'You bring me the hatchet and the bayonet we buried,' he whispered to them. 'Make sure no one sees you, all right?'

A marine captain walked over to them. Davies hurried off to the beach. The captain was young with gentle features. He was short and wore black leather boots and white trousers. He stuck his chest out and held his hands behind his back.

'My name is Captain Tench,' he announced. 'I shall be guarding the farm today.'

'I feel safer already, sir,' replied Barrett.

Tench looked at Barrett. Was Barrett making fun of him? But he couldn't think of anything to say. Instead he spoke to Jacob.

'The Governor wants to speak to you,' he said.

'Why?' Jacob was worried.

'Report to his quarters and he will tell you!' ordered Tench.

Jacob stood at the entrance of the Governor's tent. A group of carpenters were busy nearby, building a house for the Governor. But for now Jacob had no door to knock upon. A white greyhound trotted out between the canvas flaps and stared at Jacob.

'Come in!' called the Governor from within.

It might have been a tent but inside it looked like a house. There was a dining table, rugs, a washbasin, pictures, a mirror and even a wooden bed. The Governor was sitting behind a desk reading a letter. The greyhound trotted back in past Jacob and lay down beside the Governor's chair. Jacob felt as if he was in England again, standing before a wealthy master.

'You fought off the natives yesterday,' said the Governor.

'It was more William Davies than me, sir,' replied Jacob.

'I expect it was,' said the Governor. 'But I want you to understand that I don't want a war with the natives. We have to learn from them. They have been living here some time. How is the farm getting on?'

'Slowly, sir,' said Jacob.

'Why?' asked the Governor.

'The soil, sir, it's no good,' Jacob explained. 'And even though it's February the ground is baked hard by the sun. Then there are all kinds of rats. They come at night and dig up what we have planted.'

'You're a farmer, aren't you?' asked the Governor, getting to his feet.

'I am,' answered Jacob. Then he said, 'There's something I wanted to ask.'

The Governor sighed.

'I was transported for seven years,' said Jacob, determined to ask his question. 'But I spent five years in prison before being put on a ship, and it took nearly a year to get here, so—'

'Enough!' shouted the Governor. 'You're the only farmer I have. Most of the men here have

never seen a day's work. You have to make this
farm work, so I'm going to put you in charge
there. I want the others to know you're in
charge, so you are not to wear that convict
shirt any more. And when you have made
that land grow crops, then, and only then,
will we talk about when you might go home.'

Jacob was given a pale blue shirt to wear,
like the brick-master and the blacksmith. He
then made his way to the farm. As soon as
Barrett and the others saw him they stopped
work. They saw his new shirt and looked at
each other in surprise. Barrett spat on the
ground in disgust.

'Come here, all of you,' said Captain Tench,
who must have felt the need to say something.

The men dropped their tools and walked
towards Tench.

'The Governor has put Jones in charge of the
farm,' he told them. 'I want you all to follow
his orders. If you don't, you will be flogged.
Now get on with your work.'

Everyone was looking at Jacob. All his life he
had taken orders. For the first time ever he had
to give them. He looked at the hungry, tired
faces. How could he inspire them to work?

'Hard as it is, we have to make this land feed us,' he said. 'Some of the officers, and people back in England, expect us to fail out here. Maybe you do. But the truth is, we can't afford to. We are going to make a farm. We have to plant deep, water the ground every day, clear the ground of roots and stones. Let's get on with it.'

There was silence.

Then Tench shouted, 'You heard the man!'

The men worked. Perhaps a convict giving orders meant something different to them. They worked all day. As the sun was beginning to go down, Barrett suddenly cried out in pain.

'I've been bitten, Captain!' Barrett shrieked, hopping on one leg and holding his other ankle. 'A snake's got me! Oh God, no!'

Jacob knew that he had to take control. He helped Barrett to walk over to the gum tree to sit in the shade. It was a nasty bite. He decided he needed to get Barrett back to camp to get treatment. But before they left, he dug up the buried hatchet and put it down the back of his trousers.

That evening, when Jacob sat down with other men to eat, they moved away. He noticed how

the brick-master was also sitting alone. He
realized that there was a price to pay for being
in charge.

Jacob wondered what his wife, Susannah, was
doing back in England. He wondered what his
daughter would look like now.

'How do you like being a master, then?'

It was William Davies who had spoken to him.

'I don't like it. How do you like the fishing
party?' asked Jacob.

'Home from home, Jacob,' replied Davies.
'You got what I asked for?'

'I buried the hatchet on the beach,' said
Jacob. 'I'll show you later.'

'Good boy,' said Davies. 'Where's the bayonet?'

Jacob was not ready to answer that question
yet. He knew that the bayonet was still buried
by the gum tree.

Instead he asked: 'What I want to know is,
what do you need them for?'

'I'm going to be leaving,' whispered Davies.
'You bring me that bayonet and I promise I'll
take you with me.'

Jacob looked at the sea and saw the fin of a
dolphin disappearing into the water.

What do you think?

How can the Governor stop people stealing from the food stores?

How do you think Jacob feels about being in charge of other convicts? How might the other convicts feel? Why might a convict giving orders mean something different to the men?

Jacob needs to convince the convicts to work as a team. What's hard about teamwork?

3

The hunting party

It was finally Sunday. The day of rest. A day when marines had to clean their kit and convicts returned to building their own huts from wood and bark. Jacob was too tired to do much at all. He decided to visit Barrett in the hospital tent. He felt that this was what someone in charge should do. On his way there he met the Governor and Captain Tench.

'We've been looking for you,' said the Governor. 'How would you like to go hunting with Captain Tench?'

Jacob knew that this was not really a question. He had no choice but to agree.

'Hunting, sir?' asked Jacob.

'Yes, you must have done some poaching back in England,' said Tench.

'A little, sir,' Jacob admitted.

'Right, well, off you go with Tench, then,' ordered the Governor.

The hunting party set off in a small boat. They went deep into the bay and then upstream along the river.

Jacob rowed the boat carrying Tench and two marines. One was just a young lad called Sam. The other was a man from Scotland called Ferguson. He had a patch over one eye and was old enough to be Sam's father. A strange hunting party, thought Jacob. In the bottom of the boat was a length of rope.

'It reminds me of the River Thames at Putney. Don't you think so?' asked Tench.

'I don't know, sir. I've never been to London,' Jacob answered.

Jacob rowed for over an hour. Ferguson had fallen asleep at one end of the boat.

'Captain, Captain!' Sam suddenly shouted. 'Look! Smoke, sir! Smoke!'

Tench shook Ferguson awake.

'Row to the shore,' he told Jacob.

They headed slowly towards the smoke. When they got to the fire there was no one there.

'They seem to have gone that way,' said Tench, pointing at some footprints that led into the undergrowth.

Jacob knew that something wasn't right about this hunting trip.

'Sir, what is it that we've come out here to hunt?' asked Jacob.

'Natives,' Tench said. 'The Governor wants a native. He wants to find out more about this land. He wants a native who can tell us where to find water, what we can hunt, what we can eat. He wants someone who can be a go-between with other natives. So be ready with the rope.'

Jacob was frightened. He had seen what natives could do with a spear. Ferguson smiled and Sam looked nervous. Then, behind them, there was the sound of leaves crunching underfoot and a flash of movement.

A native woman sprinted through the undergrowth. Sam ran after her and Jacob followed him.

'Don't shoot her!' Tench yelled after the marine.

The young woman jumped over shrubs. In seconds she was running along the river bank. By now Jacob and Sam were closing on her. She looked over her shoulder and screamed.

Sam took longer strides and reached out his arm for her shoulder.

Before Sam could grab hold of her, Jacob kicked out with his leg and tripped Sam up.

Sam fell flat on his face and Jacob stopped running. The native girl was gone. Tench caught up with them.

'He tripped me, sir. The convict tripped me,' complained Sam.

Tench punched Jacob, knocking him to the ground.

'I didn't mean to, sir! It was an accident,' said Jacob.

'I'm warning you, do something like that again and I'll shoot you,' Tench said.

They went back to the camp and built up the fire. Jacob was sent to collect firewood and leaves. Ferguson shot a crow and began to cut away the wings and pluck off the feathers. When he had finished he made a spit to cook it on. That evening they ate the cooked crow. The meat was tough and bitter. And one crow was not much between four hungry men.

As they sat by the fire Ferguson and Sam talked about some of the women convicts at the settlement. Their language embarrassed Tench and made Jacob fearful for the women's safety.

Early the next morning Captain Tench was on his feet kicking the others awake.

'Are we following those footprints, sir?' asked Sam.

'No, we are not. I want this fire built up. And I want you to go and kill something that somebody would want to eat. Get going,' ordered Tench.

Sam jumped to his feet. Tench kicked him up the backside and the boy fled into the trees beyond.

'We're staying here,' Tench said to the other two men. 'Our prey will come to us if we have something they want. We need more firewood. Get on with it.'

As the sun climbed high in the sky they heard shot after shot from Sam's gun in the distance. Finally, Sam returned with what looked like a small kangaroo. Within an hour, Ferguson had skinned it and chopped it up. Large cuts of it were put onto the fire.

'I heard that the meat is good,' said Ferguson.

'I want the air filled with the smell of it,' ordered Tench.

Jacob turned the meat on the fire. Ferguson and Sam stood guard with their muskets ready. Tench sat on the ground, whistling.

'Put down your muskets, but be ready with your bayonets,' Tench said to his men.

They were not keen but they did as they were ordered. The hunting party waited and waited. They felt as though they were being watched but they could not see anyone. Then, as if by magic, without the sound of a footstep, a native was standing over Tench.

The native pointed to the fire and the food. Perhaps he thought the white men had come in peace. Or perhaps he was hungry enough to take a risk. He held out a wooden club as if he was willing to exchange it for some meat.

'Give the man some food,' said Tench calmly, slowly getting to his feet.

Jacob held out some meat on the end of a sharpened stick. The native moved closer and took the meat. Tench nodded at Ferguson and Sam, ordering them to attack. Within a split-second there were two bayonets at the native's throat.

'Get the rope!' Tench shouted to Jacob. Tench grabbed the native by the arms.

Jacob didn't move. He didn't like what they were doing.

So Tench took the rope and tied the native's arms behind his back. They took the native to the boat and shoved him in. As Jacob rowed away, he saw a woman watching from the shore. She was the woman they had chased the day before.

What do you think?

Why has the Governor chosen Jacob to go hunting with Tench?

Why do you think Jacob trips the young marine up? Why do Jacob and Tench feel differently about taking a native Australian prisoner?

How should we react if someone in authority asks us to do something that we don't agree with?

4

We reap what we sow

By midday the hunting party and their prisoner were back in the settlement. Jacob's shoulders ached from rowing the boat. Some men could row all day and then do the same the next day. They were used to it. Jacob was not. But as soon as they had delivered the native prisoner to the Governor, Jacob and Tench were sent to the farm.

When Jacob reached the farm Barrett walked over to meet him. He was limping badly from the snake bite. His ankle had swollen up like an orange. He looked pale.

'They said you had gone hunting. Did you bring back any meat?' Barrett asked.

Jacob shook his head.

'What did you catch? You must have caught something,' Barrett moaned.

Jacob was looking past Barrett to the ground that they had cleared and sown. He could see green shoots. He pushed past Barrett and bent

down. The barley seeds they had planted had
begun to sprout. Jacob held one between his
fingers and pulled it gently. The tiny roots were
close to the surface. The sandy soil fell away
and the plant came up easily.

Then Jacob felt a hand on his shoulder.
Tench was standing next to him.

'Great news,' said Tench, looking at the
new plants with a smile. 'The Governor will
be delighted.'

Jacob realized that Tench thought he was
looking at a miracle. Tench could see a harvest
ahead. But Jacob knew better. He had spent all
his young life working on farms and he knew
that the crop did not look healthy. Large red
ants crawled about the cracks in the earth.

'When you have finished here today, report
to the Governor,' Tench said. 'Tell him the good
news.'

Jacob said nothing to Tench but he knew that
it was not really good news. It would not be
long before the shoots died. He told Barrett and
the others to water every little plant. He ordered
them to clear more ground too. He made sure
that everyone was busy right until the end of
the day.

While they were working he dug up the bayonet by the gum tree. On the way back to the settlement he buried it on the beach.

As Jacob waited outside the Governor's tent he could see the native prisoner tied to a post nearby. Duggan, the marine who had been speared in the leg at the farm, was guarding him. Jacob saw Duggan kick his captive and spit in his face.

'What do you want?' said the Governor, surprised to see Jacob.

'Captain Tench told me to tell you that we have some barley shoots on the farm,' said Jacob.

'Wonderful news!' exclaimed the Governor, getting to his feet. 'How long before we have a crop?'

Jacob said nothing for a moment or two.

'Sir,' he said finally, 'I don't think there will ever be a crop. Not with that poor soil.'

'There has to be a crop, you understand,' said the Governor. Now he sounded upset and angry. 'There has to be!'

Jacob took in a breath. He knew that this might not be the best time, but he had to take his chances when he could. 'Sir, have you given any more thought to how long I will be here for? What with my time nearly being up?' he asked.

'To be honest, I don't know,' said the Governor. 'There are no records here. I have been given no information about how long any convict is here for. As far as I know you are all here for life.'

Jacob bowed his head and left the tent. The native's eyes met his as Jacob passed by. They seemed to ask for mercy.

That evening as Jacob was eating, Davies came up to him.

'You got the bayonet?' Davies asked.

'Same place as the hatchet,' replied Jacob.

'Good,' Davies said. 'We'll go tomorrow night,' he promised.

Jacob nodded. He decided that before then there was something he wanted to do.

After dark he crept out of his tent and dug up the bayonet on the beach. Then he headed straight for the Governor's tent. It was so dark that he didn't bother to hide his weapon. The native was asleep, with one arm tied to the post with a rope. He was wearing a marine's red coat. He must have been given it to keep him warm at night on the Governor's orders. Jacob had expected to see Duggan guarding him, but Duggan wasn't there.

Jacob quickly woke the native and put his finger on his lips to show him to be quiet. He began to cut the rope with the bayonet. Even before he had cut through, the native had pulled himself free and fled.

Jacob was about to turn and run back to his tent when he felt the barrel of a musket on the back of his head.

'That's my bayonet you've got there,' said Duggan.

Jacob heard the click as the musket was cocked.

What do you think?

Why did Jacob tell the Governor what he really thought about the farm? What else could he have done?

How do you think Jacob feels when the Governor says, 'As far as I know you are all here for life'?

Why do you think Jacob frees the native?

How should we react when we see injustice done to others? When might it be OK to do something that is wrong to protect someone else?

5

Punishment (part one)

Jacob stood before Captain Tench, the surgeon and the Governor. He was waiting to be sentenced. Jacob was certainly guilty. They just had to decide what the punishment would be. The surgeon looked worried.

'Why did you do it? Why did you release the native?' asked the Governor angrily.

'I don't see why he should be a prisoner when this is his home,' answered Jacob.

The Governor slammed his fist on the table.

'Dammit, man, he was important to us! We need to know what they know about this land,' he said.

'I am sorry, sir,' Jacob said quietly.

'We should remember that what Jacob did was an act of kindness,' the surgeon said. 'He didn't seek to gain from it.'

'It's ruined our plans all the same,' said Tench.

The Governor sat for a moment. He was clearly deciding how tough to be on the man who had taken away their hope of finding out how to survive in this strange land.

'I would say no more than a hundred lashes, sir,' suggested the surgeon. 'He is our farmer.'

Jacob's mouth dried. He looked at the men sitting in judgement on him. Was anyone going to suggest less than a hundred? Then he had a terrifying thought. *What if they said more?*

'A hundred lashes it is,' said the Governor.

Jacob was led away and his legs placed in irons to prevent him from running away. There had been several floggings in the first few weeks. Even to watch them was too much to bear. Jacob had never been keen on church but that night he needed to pray. There was no chaplain in the settlement, so the surgeon led the men in prayer and took funerals. The surgeon had seemed sympathetic to him, so Jacob asked to see him and they prayed together.

Jacob was led out the next morning. As usual all the convicts were made to watch the punishment. A well-built corporal was shaking out the whip. The 'cat', as it was known, was nine strips of leather with lead shot melted into the ends of the strips.

Jacob had watched William Davies get flogged. He had taken a hundred lashes for answering back to a major once too often. Davies had not made a sound as they flicked the flesh off his back. After one hundred lashes he had walked over to his woman, standing straighter than the Governor. Now Davies was in the front row to watch Jacob.

In front of Jacob were three stakes pushed into the ground to form a tripod, known as the triangle. Jacob was tied to it with his hands above his head. His feet were only just touching the ground. A leather strap was thrust into his mouth to stop him biting his tongue. There was a drum roll and his crime was read out.

'Commence punishment!' Tench commanded.

Jacob took in as much air as he could through his nose and held it. The lash cracked across his left shoulder blade.

'One,' Tench counted.

Jacob breathed out through his nose.

'Two,' Tench said.

The lash hit the same place.

After three more blows Jacob felt blood trickling down his back. After ten blows his right leg buckled. He realized that he would never make it to a hundred. The corporal moved on to his right shoulder.

The convicts watched in silence. They had seen some men flogged more than once. What mattered was how you took your punishment. The men would look down on anyone who cried out or begged the corporal to stop. Jacob knew he was being judged.

By thirty lashes the corporal had moved on to the small of his back where the skin was tightest. Insects at his feet carried pieces of flesh away. Jacob's mouth was bleeding from gripping the leather strap so tightly. He was having trouble breathing.

The surgeon raised his hand to pause the punishment. He went forward and looked at Jacob's back closely. Then he gave the signal to continue.

But after a few more strokes Jacob had passed out and was hanging off the triangle.

The punishment was stopped. There was little point in flogging a man if he couldn't feel it.

Jacob was carried off to the sick tent. He was laid face down on the floor and the surgeon threw a bucket of water with vinegar mixed in it across his back.

Jacob woke up.

'That will teach you to look after the natives,' said the surgeon. 'I put some vinegar in the water. It stings but it stops infection. Here, chew on these. They will help to take the pain away.'

The surgeon handed Jacob some strips of willow bark.

'How far did I get?' asked Jacob.

'You got to fifty-two.'

The surgeon laid some large leaves across Jacob's back.

'The leaves will cool you and keep off the flies,' the surgeon told him. 'You can rest for a few days in here. Then you will need to be up and about. At some point you will have to take the other fifty lashes. But I'll hold it off as long as I can.'

Jacob felt as though his back was on fire. After the surgeon had gone Barrett came in to see him.

He asked how Jacob was. Barrett gave him some salted pork. Jacob was grateful but curious.

'Where did you get this from?' he asked.

'They gave me extra rations on account of my snake bite. Keep it quiet, though,' said Barrett.

The next morning Tench put his head in the tent.

'Roll call,' he said. 'Everyone has to be there. No exceptions.'

Jacob dragged himself outside and lined up with the other convicts and marines. As the headcount was under way Barrett limped down the line to stand next to him.

'You haven't heard, have you?' said Barrett.

'Heard what?' asked Jacob.

'Why do you think they're counting? Davies has gone. He escaped in a fishing boat with his woman.'

Last night there had been a full moon and a good tide. Davies had taken his chance. He had broken his promise to take Jacob with him and left him behind. He must have thought that the flogging would slow them down. Or maybe he thought that Jacob was going to die anyway.

What do you think?

Jacob says, 'I am sorry, sir.' What do you think Jacob is sorry for and why?

Where do you think Barrett got the extra rations from?

Why do you think Davies broke his word and left without Jacob? Should Davies have waited so that he and Jacob could escape together? Why? How important is 'keeping your word'?

6

Punishment (part two)

Two days later Jacob reported for duty at the farm. Jacob knew that they would not continue with his flogging for a few days at least. And he trusted the surgeon to give him some warning.

The hot February sun beat down on the ground. Some of the shoots that had appeared had already begun to die. Still the convicts carried on planting and Tench carried on walking up and down encouraging everyone.

Jacob didn't see Barrett all day. He wondered where he was.

Late in the afternoon they returned to the settlement. As they got near they saw that the other convicts were lined up in ranks. The Governor and officers were lined up in front. Jacob and the other farm workers were ordered to join the ranks.

'Anyone who steals food steals from us all,' declared the Governor, standing on his box. 'I made the rations equal. I made this a rule so that people would not steal. I warned you all what the consequences would be. The way for us to survive in this new land is for us to work. Not to steal, not to run, but to work. We have to make the land feed us all.'

He turned towards the guardhouse. 'Captain Tench, bring out the prisoner,' he ordered.

Tench opened the guardhouse door to reveal Barrett. Barrett turned his face away from the flood of sunlight. The chains around his wrists were taken off only for his hands to be tied behind his back.

Barrett spoke two words to Tench: 'No pardon?'

Tench shook his head.

The chains around Barrett's ankles were not removed and he hobbled to where the Governor and the other convicts were waiting.

Barrett suddenly paused and gazed up. High in the sky, an eagle flew. Its wings were like two outstretched arms.

Tench saluted the Governor and led Barrett to the ladder leaning against the fig tree.

Barrett began to climb the ladder.

'Not yet, Barrett,' said Tench, grabbing him by the shoulder.

The surgeon stepped forward, his Bible open in his hands. His face was pale. He stood facing Barrett.

The surgeon read aloud the words that were used at a funeral service: '"I am the resurrection and the life. He who believes in me will live, even though he dies," says the Lord.'

He closed his Bible. Barrett turned to the ladder. Standing beside the ladder was Nichols, a convict who had worked with Barrett on the farm. Nichols walked forward and hugged Barrett. Barrett climbed a few steps up the ladder. It was leaning against a branch about ten feet off the ground. Tench followed him and fixed the noose around his neck. The bats that were roosting high up in the tree began to squeal.

There was a drum roll, then Tench ordered Nichols to pull the ladder away.

Nichols just looked back at him.

'Pull the ladder away.' Tench repeated the command.

'But, sir . . .'

Tench took a musket from a marine and pointed it at Nichols.

'If you don't pull that ladder, I will shoot you and then do it myself,' snapped Tench.

Nichols had no choice. He did what he was told. There was a great gasp among the convicts. Some fell to their knees. The bats flew away.

That evening the sky filled with heavy, dark clouds. A bolt of lightning hit a tree and set it alight. Then the rain came. It poured and poured. Jacob waited until an hour before dawn and then ran from the camp.

What do you think?

Why do you think the Governor ordered Barrett to be hanged? What other choices did he have?

Do punishments like flogging and hanging work? Why or why not?

Why has Jacob run away? What situations have you run from when you should have stayed and faced them?

7

Walkabout

Jacob headed west. East led to the ocean, north to the bay. It was the same way he had been with the hunting party, except then he had been in a boat. The moon was bright but its light did not reach through the trees. He could just make out large bats swooping above him. He could hardly see his own feet.

The ground was flat but he kept tripping over tree roots. The woods were alive with insects and night birds. Every now and then he would see pairs of red eyes glowing in the darkness.

Jacob walked until dawn but he did not get very far. He climbed a rounded rock and waited for daylight so that he could get his bearings. He could see a plume of smoke coming from further up the river. He realized that he too would have to light a fire, but first he had to find some meat to cook.

He broke a length of bamboo to use as a spear and split its end to make a point. At the base of the rocks he managed to spear a lizard. It was not much of a meal but he felt pleased with himself all the same. He gathered some sticks and dried grass and climbed back up the rocks to light a fire. He used his belt buckle to create sparks off the stone and set fire to the dried grass. Then, as he was about to begin cooking his lizard, a shadow fell on him. An eagle landed right in front of him. It placed its talon on the dead reptile. For a few seconds the eagle and Jacob looked at one another. Then the huge bird picked up the lizard in its beak and flew off.

Jacob headed north. When he reached the shore of the bay he realized how little distance inland he had travelled, for it was still salt water. But at least there was now a shoreline to walk along. He followed it as the bay narrowed to the river. The sun had climbed behind him and he was soon dizzy with thirst. He began to stop more and more often. He sat down and thought about returning to the settlement. If he did, they would probably start his flogging all over again.

Then he saw something just ahead of him on the shore. It was long, narrow and man-made. It was a canoe.

It was made out of just one large piece of bark, shaped at both ends. Its bottom was flat and there was a long paddle on board.

It didn't look strong but it did float. It seemed to Jacob that you were meant to stand up and paddle. He looked up and down the river for any sign of natives. There was no one about and no footprints in the sand.

He decided to take the canoe. He stood in its centre and paddled upstream. Soon he was past the point where he had stopped with the hunting party. He told himself that if he came across some natives he would hand the canoe over and thank them. In the meantime he had to make his way to fresh water.

He began to feel happier. Even though his back was still painful, he found himself singing. After an hour he stopped and tasted the water. It was fresh and cool. He paddled to the north shore and pulled the canoe onto the bank.

As he stepped into the water he bent down to take another drink. Then he saw a long, tube-shaped cage made of vines and held down by stones. It was a trap and there were eels in it. He had caught and eaten eels as a boy but they had been much smaller than these. He lifted the trap out of the water and looked at the eels. They were so big that their faces were the size of a puppy dog's head. He pulled one from the cage and laid it on a rock. It wriggled for its life. He was about to smash its head with a stone when a shadow fell across the ground. Behind him stood a native with a club in one hand and a spear in the other.

Jacob stood up straight and faced the man. The native was taller than him but less powerfully built. He smelt of fish oil and there were fish bones in his hair. He was entirely naked. The native smiled and Jacob noticed that there were two teeth missing from the front of his mouth. What did the smile mean? A smile of friendship? Jacob went to walk up the bank but then the tip of the spear was pressed against his chest.

'My name is Jacob,' he said, trying to sound friendly.

Out of the woods came a woman and a child. She spoke in their strange language.

The spear was pressed against Jacob again, forcing him backwards into the river. Jacob was waist-high in the water when the native drew back his spear as if to throw it at him. Jacob ducked down beneath the surface, getting a mouthful of water. When he came up a few seconds later the natives were laughing at him. The man went to throw his spear again and Jacob quickly dived underwater with no time to take a breath. He came up coughing.

His lungs were half-filled with water. He knew he could not dive down a third time and he held up his arms in surrender. Just as the native pulled the spear back over his shoulder again, Jacob saw a red jacket emerge from the woods. But it was not a marine who was wearing it. It was a native. It was the very same native Jacob had helped to escape a few nights ago.

What do you think?

Should Jacob have taken the canoe? What else could he have done?

How do you think the native Australians will treat Jacob? How might they treat him differently because Jacob helped free one of them?

Where did Jacob think he was going when he ran away? Did he have a plan?

Where do you see yourself going at present, and in the future? Do you have a plan?

8

Eel River

Jacob was led away from the river to a clearing. There was a small fire and the ground all around seemed to be scorched. A sandy-coloured dog ran beside them as they walked. Jacob's heart was beating fast, partly out of exhaustion, partly out of fear. He did not know whether he was a prisoner or a guest. Behind him the woman and the child were carrying the trapped eels. He wondered whether, if he ran, the native men would chase after him or throw the spear at him. Something told him to walk to the fire and to trust his life with these people.

The fire was built up with branches and flat stones. The eels were laid on the stones and cooked until the skin peeled away. The natives tore the heads off with their teeth. The one in the red jacket handed Jacob the bloody remains of one.

'Parramatta,' he said. Jacob thought that must be their word for eel.

45

There was only enough eel meat for one or two mouthfuls each when it was divided among the four adults and the child. But the food had been shared and Jacob showed them how grateful he was.

He repeated his name several times, pointing to himself: 'Jacob, Jacob.'

'Jacob, Jacob,' they said back to him.

Jacob discovered that the man in the marine's jacket was called Bennelong. The other man's name was Daku and the woman's name was Hanya.

Bennelong led Jacob to the trees. He cut down a thin branch and tried out its balance as a spear. He then gave it to Jacob to try. Jacob held it above his shoulder. He had never thrown or even held a spear before and he enjoyed the feel of it in his hands.

Then Bennelong showed Jacob how to make a sharpened tip with shells. The branch, which must have been six feet long, was stripped of its bark and hardened over the fire.

As it began to get dark the group headed south from the river to hunt. The small child, who was Daku and Hanya's son, ran ahead and checked bird traps. These were mounds of earth with tunnels dug into them that led to a dead end. The natives put berries in the tunnels, and the birds would enter to eat the berries, but then find that there was no room for them to turn around to get out. The native people knew that birds can't walk backwards. The boy held up a blackbird, then broke its neck with a twist of his wrist.

Further on, Bennelong climbed up some pinkish rocks and waved to Jacob to follow him. Bennelong and Jacob lay flat on their stomachs, with head and shoulders hanging over the edge of the rocks. Below them on the ground, Daku and Hanya and their boy were hiding behind some bushes. Jacob was nervous. What were they waiting for? Whoever, or whatever, it was, Jacob knew that he was expected to throw his spear.

Just as it was getting dark, a huge bird like a turkey came running into view, followed by another, then another. Bennelong looked to where Daku was hiding. When Daku waved his arm Bennelong launched his spear down into the back of the last bird. It halted for a moment but then carried on. Then Jacob stood and threw his spear into the bird. It fell to the ground. Bennelong jumped down next to it.

'Emu. Emu,' Bennelong told Jacob, pointing at the bird to make himself understood.

They ate the bird over two days. In that time Jacob came to realize that Daku and Bennelong were brothers. But he noticed that there was some tension between them. Although Jacob had no idea what they were saying, it was easy to tell when people were arguing in any language.

Then the group moved further up the river. They arrived at a place where the river widened like a pool. On one bank of the river there were mangrove trees. On the other side of the river there was long grass, where ducks had nested. Jacob saw the remains of some old nests. The nests were empty, and the ducks were bobbing up and down in the river. Jacob hid in the long grass with Daku, Hanya and the boy, and they watched the ducks.

Meanwhile, Bennelong had doubled back across the river into the mangrove trees. Jacob began to wonder how they would kill the ducks. Bennelong might spear one but then the rest would fly away, and one duck would not feed them all. Jacob looked to Daku for clues. There was no bow and arrow and they were too far away to hit such a small target with a spear.

Daku just sat, looking out onto the river. He tapped the ground with a curved piece of wood that Jacob had seen him carving over the last few days.

Then Bennelong jumped from the mangrove trees towards them, scaring the ducks into the air. In a flash, Daku was on his feet. He swung his arm and threw the curved piece of wood, making it spin high into the air. The wood spun towards the ducks and hit one of the flock. The duck dropped to the earth. The weapon spun back towards Daku, landing nearby. He collected it and the boy ran to pick up the bird.

Bennelong had also struck with his spear at the same time as Daku. He waded back across the river with a duck on the end of his spear.

As they waited for the two birds to cook over the fire Jacob picked up the strange weapon Daku had used to bring down the duck. It was shaped like the corner of a table, a few inches wide, flat on one side, raised on the other. He turned it in his hand the way it turned in the air.

'Boomerang. Boomerang,' Daku said, taking it from him.

Then Daku led him to the mangrove trees on the other side of the river, carrying his stone axe.

Daku cut down and split the base of a tree. On some rocks he chopped out the shape of the boomerang. They went back to the camp and Daku began working the wood.

Jacob could see that this would take some time. It would take great skill to make a piece of wood that you could throw and that would spin back to you. He watched Daku use the axe and stone to shape the wood.

Suddenly Bennelong became angry again. At first Jacob wasn't sure whether he was shouting at him or at Daku. Then Bennelong held his hands together as if they were tied, pointing at Jacob. Then he pointed at Hanya, all the time talking excitedly. It was clear that he was telling a story. It was the story of how, in the few days that he had been held prisoner by the marines, his wife had been taken by another man. Of course, Jacob couldn't be sure, but he looked at Bennelong and recognized someone who had lost a wife.

After this everyone was silent. They went to sleep on the long grass. Jacob had stopped worrying about what crawled over him when he lay down. He had learned that insects and lizards weren't interested in killing him. Like him, they were only interested in surviving.

He noticed that he could see many more stars in the night sky than he ever could in England.

What do you think?

Why have Bennelong and Daku taken Jacob with them and taught him to hunt?

Do you think that Jacob is better or worse off with Bennelong and Daku or in the settlement with the other convicts? Why?

How easy is it for people from very different cultures to get on? What difficulties might they face?

How would you feel if you were in a wilderness?

9

Alone

The group of natives stayed in their camp by the duck pool for some time, until Jacob had lost track of the days. He couldn't remember how long it was since he had spoken to another Englishman, or even seen a white person.

One morning, when Jacob was still half-asleep, he realized that everyone else was already on their feet. The boy was playing in the river.

'Waroo,' said Bennelong, staring down at him.

It was the same word that the native had shouted that day at the farm: 'waroo'. It was a word Jacob now knew the meaning of. It meant 'go'.

The family walked off, the boy running to catch up with them. Jacob did not try to follow. He watched them follow the river. Perhaps Bennelong felt that he had now repaid Jacob for releasing him from the marines. Or perhaps being with Jacob reminded him of how he had lost his wife. Either way, Jacob was alone in the wilderness.

At least I can find food and water, he told himself. He looked around, in all directions. The fire was out but they had left the fire sticks, which were still glowing. He had a spear and he had the boomerang Daku had made for him. He went to hunt.

He sat in the long grass peering out towards the ducks. No one was going to send them in his direction. He crawled along the ground with his spear by his side, as near to the ducks as he dared. He had seen Bennelong throw his spear a hundred yards and hit a narrow hardwood tree. Jacob had tried to do the same, and they had laughed when his spear landed well short of the tree.

Jacob knew that a farmer had to be patient but it was nothing like the patience that a hunter needed. He lay chest down on the ground waiting for a duck to drift close to his side of the river. A few came nearer. He picked one out, took aim and threw. The bird was gone before his spear hit the spot where it had swum. His spear sank.

He fetched his boomerang, went back to his place and waited again. He sat still for two hours. His shoulders were badly burnt by the sun and his lips were cracked with dryness. His tongue was stuck to the roof of his mouth. At last the flock of ducks returned. He threw a pebble into the ducks to scare them into the air. With his other arm he swung the boomerang into the flock. It didn't spin, it didn't hit any of the ducks, and it didn't come back.

Jacob set off back to where he had first met Bennelong and the others. His plan was to make some eel traps like the one he had found. He twisted some vines together to make the narrow baskets, put them in place and sat on the river bank.

He thought of the stream running through the farm where he had worked back in England. All the workers would sit there after harvest and the farmer would bring out great big jugs of cider for them. That was how he had met his wife, Susannah. She was a servant girl. He had watched her carry out the large jug, the sunlight shining on her long blonde hair. All the labourers had tried to catch her eye but it was only Jacob she had spoken to. She said just three words: 'Enjoy your cider.'

The following morning he had gone round to ask if he could walk with her to church, and she had accepted. Within a year they were married. She was already several months pregnant on their wedding day.

He got up to check his traps. Suddenly he heard voices, English voices.

'If you see one, wave. Understand? We come in friendship.'

Jacob darted behind a tree. A boat was being rowed up the river. It was the Governor and two marines.

'Any sign?' the Governor shouted.

As the boat got closer, one of the marines peered over the side.

'Sir, sir!' the marine called. He jumped out of the boat into the water and lifted up one of Jacob's eel traps.

'It's a fish trap. They must be round here somewhere, sir,' he said.

'Let's get ashore,' ordered the Governor.

They rowed to the far bank. They got out of the boat and began to head into the woods.

Jacob was afraid. If he went back to the settlement he would certainly be flogged again.

He would possibly also be punished further for having run away. But greater than his fear of being flogged was his fear of being stuck in the wilderness alone.

Jacob watched as the Governor began to disappear from view. Then he made his decision. He came out from behind the tree and walked down to the river.

'Sir! Sir! It is I, Jacob Jones,' he shouted at the top of his voice.

The Governor turned and came back to the shore.

'Jones? Jacob Jones the farmer?' he asked.

'Yes, sir. And that is my eel trap,' Jacob explained.

'You are hunting eels, are you?' said the Governor. 'We're hunting natives again, thanks to you.'

'There are no natives around here, sir,' said Jacob. He was not sure if this was true, but he did not want to put Bennelong's family at risk. 'I've been living with some natives for these past weeks, but they have moved on now.'

'You've been living with them, have you? Well, you can come back to the settlement and tell me all about it,' the Governor ordered.

What do you think?

Do you think Jacob is pleased to see the
    Governor? Why? What do you think the
    Governor feels when he sees Jacob?

Do you think that Jacob would have
    survived alone? Why do you think Jacob
    decided to turn himself in?

What is it like to be lonely?

10

Another chance

Jacob was once again standing before the Governor. This time he was in the main room of the Governor's newly built house. It wasn't grand, but it was the first house in the settlement. There was furniture there that had not been in the tent. The Governor must have been keeping it in his ship, which was still moored in the port. There was a fireplace with a mantelpiece and a clock that ticked and chimed. He had a red and green parrot that nodded on its perch.

The Governor was making tea. Outside someone was being flogged. Jacob flinched a little with each crack of the whip.

'You lasted longer than the others out there,' said the Governor, sipping his tea.

'The natives looked after me, sir,' replied Jacob.

'Ah, your friends the natives.' The Governor snorted. 'I heard it wasn't easy capturing the native. You took it upon yourself to release him, and then you ran away from the farm.'

'No, sir, I ran away from a flogging,' Jacob explained.

The Governor stared hard at Jacob, trying to decide whether he was telling the truth.

'And now you're back,' he said. 'People always come back. Tell me, where did you go with the natives?'

'About a day's walk from where you found me, sir,' Jacob said. 'The river opens up. There are plenty of ducks to eat and the soil is good. Like back home.'

The Governor finished his tea. Jacob heard the last lash on some poor soul's back. An officer shouted, 'Punishment complete.'

'The farm at the settlement won't feed us,' the Governor said. 'You were right about that. And the livestock we brought with us have run off or else been killed by the natives. So I've sent Captain Tench to the Cape of Africa to buy grain and livestock. But he won't be back for weeks. I fear the convicts may rebel. I'm going to send you back.'

'To England, sir?' asked Jacob hopefully.

'No, to where I found you,' said the Governor. 'Where you say the soil is good. Plough the earth there. Grow some food.

I'm giving you another chance. If you grow me some food, you will not have to suffer the remaining fifty lashes.'

'Thank you, sir,' Jacob said. He was so relieved. He could not believe it. He had escaped the rest of the flogging and he was not going to be punished for running away.

'Sir, can I say something?' asked Jacob.

He knew that he should get out while he could, but the thought of what he owed to Bennelong and Daku meant that he felt he had to try and say something.

'I'm not sure you should take the natives prisoner,' Jacob went on. 'We can learn more from them if we spend time living with them.'

The Governor raised his eyebrows.

'Don't push your luck, Jones,' he said, pointing to the door.

The next day, Jacob, Private Duggan, another marine and a party of convicts rowed up the river. The Governor had decided to name the river the Parramatta after the native word for eels. They landed where Jacob had met Bennelong and followed Jacob to the clearing.

The Governor had made it clear that Jacob was in charge of the farm. People were given tents, tools and some food supplies. They were expected to look out for themselves. Anyone who refused to work was to be sent back to the main settlement.

On the first morning Jacob told the group that no huts would be built until the land had been planted. He ordered them to clear the grass, then to chop down some trees to be burned. The wood ash was dug in to improve the soil. Jacob wanted to give this land the best chance he could. He knew that the future of the settlement depended on them. The next morning he called everyone together.

'I'm going out to do some hunting,' he announced. 'I need someone to come with me.'

Private Duggan limped forward carrying his musket.

'I don't need a gun for what I've got in mind,' he told Duggan, shaking his head.

From the back of the group, a woman spoke up.

'I was transported for poaching game,' she said. 'I'm used to hunting in the dead of night.'

'We are not hunting rabbits,' said Jacob.

'Most animals leave tracks,' she said. 'They think with their noses.'

'What's your name?' asked Jacob.

'Eliza Worley.'

Jacob reckoned she was in her late teens. She was small and stocky with a pretty face. She stood with her hands on her hips, waiting for his answer.

'All right, come with me now if you like,' he said.

Eliza walked beside Jacob as he led her to the river bank. He showed her how to make eel traps.

'You ever tickled a trout?' he asked her.

She nodded.

'When you have finished making these traps, see if you can land me a fish,' Jacob instructed.

'For supper, is it?' she asked hopefully.

'No,' Jacob said. 'For its teeth.'

Later Jacob cut down some branches to make two spears. He fixed oyster shells at their tips and fish teeth in the sides as barbs.

They headed off west, away from the river for about five miles. It was the place where he had hunted with Bennelong. He knew that the bird he was after returned there from time to time. It was an area of rocks, sand and water holes. Some of the water holes were pools big enough to bathe in. He checked the tracks in the sand and tried to work out how many birds had come this way. He led Eliza away from the tracks to a hiding place behind a deep green bush.

'I want you to hide here,' he told her. 'I'll be up on the rocks. When the last one comes through, wave to me.'

'The last what?' she asked.

'You'll see,' he said.

They waited nearly three hours. Jacob had expected this, but Eliza began to fidget. Maybe she wondered whether this mystery animal existed. Then a group of emus came around the base of the rocks. Jacob lay flat on his belly on the rocks across from Eliza. She was amazed at their size and stood in front of the bush to get a good look at them. The great birds were aware of her presence and began to stride on faster.

'Now!' Eliza yelled as the last bird passed under Jacob.

He flung his spear down into the bird's back and it collapsed. It tried to raise itself, but Eliza cut off its head with the hatchet to end its suffering. Jacob jumped down.

'Always hunt these birds from on high,' he told her. 'They can't look up. And only hunt the last one. The ones in front can't look behind them, so they will come back this way again, following their own tracks and not knowing there's any danger.'

The bird was roasted over a spit and the eels were cooked in a pan. The convicts enjoyed the fresh meat and fish. Progress had been made on turning the soil, although some men were already complaining about the work.

Jacob decided that this place would need a name. Someone joked that perhaps it should be called 'Jacob' since there was a 'Sydney' down the road. He told them about the eels, about the Eel People, and about how the Governor had named the river the Parramatta, after the native word for eels.

'So this,' he told them all, 'is now called Parramatta Farm.'

What do you think?

Why do you think the Governor gave Jacob a chance to escape the remainder of his punishment? Did you expect him to do this, or did you expect something else?

Why did Jacob try and persuade the Governor not to take more natives prisoner? Was he right to do this?

How do you think Jacob feels now that the other convicts are depending on him to make the farm a success? How do you feel when someone is depending on you for something?

11

Parramatta Farm

Six months later the farm was going well. Jacob now understood the seasons in Australia. Winter here was as warm as an English summer but compared to the other seasons it was a winter. If the soil was good enough there could be two harvests in a year.

They had cleared and ploughed more than fifty acres, and dug ditches. He and Eliza had built themselves a small cabin. The cabin was made of wood on three sides and brick on the other side. It had two rooms and a fireplace with a mantelpiece. There were kangaroo hides on the floor and a boomerang hanging over the fireplace. There were shutters at the windows but no glass. It was the first house at Parramatta.

They had already grown a crop of beetroot, potatoes and green beans. Jacob was planning to plant a wheat field.

There was now a track between the settlement at Sydney Cove and Jacob's farm. But when the

Governor visited he still preferred to come by boat. He arrived one morning with Captain Tench.

Tench had recently returned with supplies from the Cape of Africa. He looked thin and pale, and he seemed to have aged.

'Do you think the wheat will grow?' the Governor asked.

'I believe it will grow waist-high, sir,' said Jacob with a smile. 'Just like in Kent.'

The Governor nodded and sent Tench to get something from the boat.

'A gift for you,' said the Governor. Tench returned, carrying six small trees. 'Apple trees, Jacob. They're from the Cape. It seems a nice place for an orchard.'

'Thank you, sir.'

The Governor took a few paces towards Jacob's cabin.

'It looks sturdy enough,' he said, smacking his hand on the cabin wall.

'And I have dug a well, sir,' said Jacob with a touch of pride.

'We have some window glass on one of the supply ships,' the Governor continued. 'I'll let you have some.'

Jacob brought the Governor inside his cabin. Jacob sat on a bench and the Governor sat on a stool.

'Tell me, Jacob, do the farmhands out there know what they're doing?' he asked.

'I think so,' Jacob answered. 'Most do anyway.'

'They could carry on without you,' the Governor said. 'So, if you wish, you can have your passage home to England now. What with time in prison and time spent out here, your sentence has long passed. As of now, you're a free man.'

'When does the ship sail?' Jacob asked excitedly.

'Soon. But I want to offer you another choice,' said the Governor.

'Sir?'

'A land grant,' the Governor said. 'It will be the first in the colony. I'll give you thirty acres to begin with. Of this farm.'

Jacob looked out through the open door. He divided up thirty acres in his mind's eye. He would need help to work the land.

'I could sell the grain to you, could I?' Jacob asked.

'You could,' said the Governor with a smile. 'And you're still free to go home at any time.'

Eliza had returned from hunting and was talking to Tench.

'I'm going to offer land to others too,' the Governor explained. 'The government back in London wants the land settled. Who knows what it will become in time. Have a think, Jacob. If you want to go back to being a farmhand in England, the ship leaves in three days.'

The Governor left. He called to Tench to follow him as if he was calling to one of his dogs.

Jacob looked at the promise of the land. It was good land. It was high enough above the river to avoid flooding. It was easy to drain if need be. The soil was rich. He could imagine the orchard ahead of him. He looked at Eliza. She smiled and walked towards him. He realized that it had been a while since he had thought about his wife in England, Susannah, and their child.

'Why are you looking so serious, Jacob Jones?' asked Eliza.

'The Governor is going to give us some glass so we can have windows,' he said.

'And you're unhappy about that, are you?' she asked.

Jacob did not reply. Instead he suggested that they go for a walk.

'What did the Governor want with you?' Eliza asked, determined to have some answers.

'He came to tell me that I could take a ship home,' Jacob said. 'What did Tench want with you?'

'He wants to go hunting with me,' she said. 'Are you going home?'

He pulled at a blade of grass and then chewed it.

'The Governor is giving me thirty acres of this land,' he told her. 'I will own it. I never owned land in England and I never will. Besides, you've another year to do here. So, it looks like I'll be staying.'

'That's just as well,' said Eliza with a broad smile, 'because I'm carrying your child.'

What do you think?

Why does Tench look so unwell?

Why do you think Jacob hasn't thought much of his wife and child in England? What do you think may have happened to them without a husband or father?

Why do you think Jacob decided to stay in Australia rather than go home? What would it be like to have to set up home in another country?

12

Home

Two years later, Jacob held his young son's hand tightly as he led him to the edge of the river. The toddler stared down at the cool water around his toes. He looked up at his father and smiled.

It was early morning and there was a mist rolling downstream. In recent months Jacob had seen thick smoke above the distant mountains. The gum trees were known to catch fire by themselves. He had also learned that the natives set fire to them to clear ground to allow new growth.

Eliza waved from the house. Jacob lifted Matthew up to wave back to his mother. The cabin was bigger now. It was a house, in fact. There were brick walls at both ends, and proper windows. Inside, there was a stove, table and chairs. The settlement at Sydney was trading and a second fleet of marines and convicts had arrived with supplies. Eliza walked over to Jacob and her son.

'Try a mouthful of this cider,' she said, handing Jacob a cup.

Jacob took a gulp and gave a big smile.

'And keep Matthew away from the river, will you,' she said.

Just then they heard shouting from the fields. It was their neighbour, Duggan, running towards them, dragging his injured leg. Although he had left the marines to become a sheep farmer Duggan still thought of himself as a marine. He no longer wore the red coat but he still had the striped trousers and marine issue boots. He was also carrying his musket.

'Jacob, Jacob! Have you seen? Have you seen?' Duggan shouted, pointing to his farm up the hill.

'Seen what, Duggan?' asked Jacob.

'Natives, Jacob, natives!'

'Where?'

'On my land!' yelled Duggan.

There was a thin plume of smoke at the end of Duggan's nearest field. Jacob strode towards it and Duggan followed.

'Aren't you getting your gun, Jacob?' asked Duggan.

Jacob did not reply.

As they got closer it became clear that there was a small family group around a fire. Duggan held back as Jacob walked slowly towards them. He saw Bennelong and his clan. There was Daku and Hanya, with two children now, and someone new. It was a young woman, heavily pregnant.

Jacob walked forward to greet Bennelong. Bennelong introduced Jacob to his new wife, remembering Jacob's name as if it was only yesterday they had seen each other. Then he seemed to tell his wife the story of their meeting and of their time together.

Daku's boy was now old enough to be carrying a spear.

They were cooking a crow on the fire. Jacob remembered eating crow. It was bitter. And one crow would not go far between six people. Jacob pointed down the slope to his house and invited everyone to follow him.

Duggan went back to his own cabin.

Eliza was waiting at the door. She carried Matthew in her arms. Jacob introduced the clan one by one and brought them into the house.

'Jacob, what are you doing?' Eliza whispered.

'There is no need to whisper,' he told her. 'They don't understand English.'

They all sat down on the floor.

'Eliza, heat up the stew for them,' Jacob said.

'That was meant for us,' she complained.

'They fed me when I was starving,' replied Jacob.

While Eliza cooked a meal, Bennelong and Jacob spoke to one another as far as they could. The others explored the house. Daku lifted the rough boomerang that Jacob had made himself off the wall over the fireplace, looked at it and laughed. Then he took his son's boomerang and gave it to Jacob. The boy didn't complain.

When the natives ate, they sat on the floor, not at the table, and they ate with their hands. Eliza was horrified when Jacob sat on the floor next to them.

'Langan?' Daku asked, holding up a piece of meat.

Jacob stood, took Daku outside and pointed to the sheep on Duggan's farm.

'Sheep, sheep,' he explained to Daku.

Daku repeated the word to himself. After they had eaten the mutton, Jacob offered everyone some cider.

'Jacob, I don't think that's a good idea,' said Eliza.

'Why? We drink it,' replied Jacob.

After the meal the natives rested on the floor, escaping the heat of the afternoon. Bennelong slept close to his new wife, with his arm around her.

Eliza called Jacob into the bedroom. They lay down together with Matthew between them.

'I'm scared,' she said.

'Why?'

'Suppose they attack us while we are asleep,' she said. 'Suppose they take Matthew? I can't tell what they are saying, or what they are thinking.'

'They won't hurt us,' he said. 'And if anyone tried, I would defend this little one with my life.'

'Perhaps we should leave,' she said. 'My time is done. We could both go home to England if we wanted.'

They slept. Outside, cockatoos chattered. In Jacob's dreams the sound became a crowd of convicts landing on the shore at Sydney Cove, crying for help.

A short time later a sound made Jacob wake up. It was a gunshot.

He jumped up and came out of the bedroom. The natives had gone. He went outside and walked in the direction of the sound. It had come from Duggan's farm. As he got closer he could see Duggan holding a musket on his shoulder. Jacob ran. He could hear Bennelong shouting. He saw the two women and the children running away. Daku was on the ground. He was bleeding from his chest.

'What have you done?' he called to Duggan.

'They killed one of my sheep!' yelled Duggan.

'They took one sheep, Duggan. You killed a man for a sheep!' shouted Jacob.

'If they take one, they will take them all,' replied Duggan.

Bennelong carried Daku to Jacob's house and they buried him beside one of the apple trees. Bennelong held a ceremony over the grave.

Jacob bowed his head and crossed himself. Even though Matthew had not seen what had happened, he was upset. He cried and wouldn't stop.

Bennelong left at sunset. Eliza and Jacob hardly spoke to each other that evening.

Finally Eliza said, 'Jacob, if you own this farm then you can sell it. With the money we get we might be able to buy a smallholding in England.'

'We have a farm right here,' he said.

'But the natives might come back. They might take our farm!' cried Eliza.

'They aren't farmers,' Jacob replied. 'Selling the farm would be like running away. I am finished with always running. When the natives come here we will be kind to them. We need to get used to living alongside them. We should share a little of what we have. We need to teach Matthew that. Some day this will be his farm. He needs to know from us that in life there is always some trouble. And it isn't solved by running away.'

They went and lay down on the bed. Eventually they fell asleep to the clicking of crickets and the soft hoot of an owl.

What do you think?

How do you think Jacob feels when he sees Bennelong and Daku again? How do you think he feels when Daku is shot?

Duggan is not arrested for killing Daku. Why do you think that is? What would happen now if there were no police to enforce the law?

Can you think of a time when you have chosen to stay and solve a problem rather than walk away from it?

Historical note

In May 1787 eleven ships set sail from England for Australia. They carried around 800 convicts and 200 marines. They arrived in January 1788 and built a settlement at what is now Sydney, the largest city in Australia. These convicts were the first to be sentenced to 'transportation' to Australia. It meant serving sentences of hard labour abroad for anything from seven years to life. Very few convicts ever came back to England. Once they had served sentences they were entitled to own land. Land was sometimes given, sometimes sold and sometimes just taken. This brought settlers into conflict with the Aboriginal people, the first Australians.

The story in this book is fiction but it is inspired by some real people. Jacob is inspired by James Ruse, who was a farm labourer sentenced to seven years' transportation for stealing two silver watches. He became the first white person, other than the British government, to own land in Australia. The site of his farm can still be seen today in Parramatta, outside Sydney.

There really was an Aboriginal man called Bennelong who was captured by the British. He escaped but later returned to live at the settlement of Sydney for several years. When the Governor returned to England, Bennelong sailed with him. He lived with the Governor in London for three years before returning to Australia.

There was also a real Captain Tench, who wrote a popular account of his time with the First Fleet in Australia.

Books available in the Star series

Not Such a Bargain
by Toby Forward (ISBN: 978 1 908713 00 1)

Josh has everything worked out. He knows how to make easy money and he's got a sweet deal living with his mum. But when he meets the lovely Lisa, she starts asking questions that don't have good answers. And soon the police are asking too.

Barcelona Away
by Tom Palmer (ISBN: 978 1 908713 01 8)

Matt likes nothing better than a couple of pints while watching football with his mates. Actually being in the stadium when the action kicks off is even better. But a match can easily turn ugly, and soon Matt will have to decide between his love for the game and his love for his daughter.

Forty-six Quid and a Bag of Dirty Washing
by Andy Croft (ISBN: 978 1 908713 02 5)

Barry is looking forward to his first days out of prison. Free at last! He has nothing to lose but his £46 discharge grant, a bag of dirty washing, and all the promises he made to himself when he was inside . . .

Bare Freedom

by Andy Croft (ISBN: 978 1 908713 03 2)

Barry is trying to get used to life on the outside. All he wants is to make up with his sister and lead a normal life. But with no money, no job and the local drug dealer after him, will Barry be able to keep out of trouble?

One Shot

by Lena Semaan (ISBN: 978 1 908713 04 9)

Dan has got his life together. He's training as a plumber and he's the star of his local boxing club. But his life hasn't always been so good. When Dan is given the chance to get revenge on his abusive dad, will he take it? After all, he'll only get one shot. Can he make it count?

Nowhere to Run

by Michael Crowley (ISBN 978 1 908713 05 6)

What's a fair punishment for stealing a watch? It's 1788 and Jacob Jones has been sentenced to seven years' labour in Australia. The work is hot, hard and dangerous. Will Jacob find a way to escape? Or is there nowhere to run?

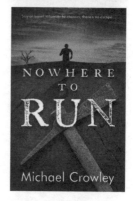

You can order these books by writing to Diffusion, SPCK, 36 Causton Street, London SW1P 4ST or visiting www.spck.org.uk/what-we-do/prison-fiction/